THE AMERICAN GIRLS

1764 KAYA, an adventurous Nez Perce girl whose deep love for horses and respect for nature nourish her spirit

1774 FELICITY, a spunky, spritely colonial girl, full of energy and independence

1824 JOSEFINA, a Hispanic girl whose heart and hopes are as big as the New Mexico sky

1854 KIRSTEN, a pioneer girl of strength and spirit who settles on the frontier

1864 ADDY, a courageous girl determined to be free in the midst of the Civil War

1904 SAMANTHA, a bright Victorian beauty, an orphan raised by her wealthy grandmother

1934 KIT, a clever, resourceful girl facing the Great Depression with spirit and determination

1944 MOLLY, who schemes and dreams on the home front during World War Two

1974 JULIE, a fun-loving girl from San Francisco who faces big changes—and creates a few of her own

1974
CHANGES FOR
Julie

BY MEGAN MCDONALD
ILLUSTRATIONS ROBERT HUNT
VIGNETTES NIKA KORNIYENKO, SUSAN MCALILEY

★American Girl®

Questions or comments? Call 1-800-845-0005, visit **americangirl.com**,
or write to Customer Service, American Girl, 8400 Fairway Place,
Middleton, WI 53562-0497.

Printed in China
07 08 09 10 11 12 LEO 10 9 8 7 6 5 4 3 2 1

PICTURE CREDITS
The following individuals and organizations have generously given
permission to reprint images contained in "Looking Back":
p. 81—courtesy Jo Freeman (campaign button); pp. 82–83—Time & Life Pictures; Newsweek;
© Owen Franken/Corbis (kids with signs); General Motors (Chevette); © Owen Franken/Corbis
(gas shortage); © H. Armstrong Roberts/Corbis (family watching TV); pp. 84–85—© Bettmann
(*Happy Days*); © Bill Pierce/Time & Life Pictures (ERA); © Leif Skoogfors/Corbis (Shirley Chisholm);
courtesy Jo Freeman (Chisholm button); © Mandel Ngan/AFP/Getty Images (Nancy Pelosi and
kids); © Matthew Cavanaugh/epa/Corbis (Pelosi button); © Mark E. Gibson/Corbis (school
library); p. 86—© Mirek Towski/Time & Life Pictures (Marlee Matlin); © Allan Tannenbaum/
Time & Life Pictures (Heather Whitestone)

Cataloging-in-Publication Data available from the Library of Congress.

IN MEMORY OF
JOHN AND MARY LOUISE MCDONALD

TABLE OF CONTENTS

CHANGES FOR JULIE

Julie's Family

Julie
*A girl full of energy
and new ideas, trying to
find her place in
times of change*

Tracy
*Julie's trendy
teenage sister, who is
sixteen years old*

Mom
*Julie's open-minded
mother, who runs a
small store*

Dad
*Julie's father,
an airline pilot who flies
all over the world*

IVY
*Julie's best friend,
who loves doing
gymnastics*

T.J.
*A boy at school
who plays basketball
with Julie*

JOY
*A new girl in Julie's class,
who lives in Julie's
neighborhood and is deaf*

STINGER
*A sixth-grade boy
who knows all about
detention*

MARK
*A popular sixth grader
running for student body
president*

DETENTION

A note!

It landed on Julie's desk in the middle of social studies class. Luckily Mrs. Duncan had her back turned as she wrote lessons on the board. Julie snatched the note and hid it in the opening of her desk. Her eyes darted around the room, making sure nobody had seen the special delivery.

Mrs. Duncan was super-strict. She always wore buttoned-up blouses that pinched her neck. Even her hair was strict—starched and stiff as a ruler. She had warned the class about passing notes. "This is fifth grade, people," she'd been saying for the first few weeks of school.

As Mrs. Duncan explained about Lewis and Clark's trip through grizzly bear country toward the Rocky Mountains, Julie snuck a peek at the note. It was from Joy Jenner, who sat across the aisle from her.

Last summer, Julie had noticed a new girl walking some of the neighborhood dogs—a Chihuahua, a toy poodle, and a cute, hairy mutt—at the park. Then, on the first day of fifth grade, there she was, in the same class! When Mrs. Duncan seated the class alphabetically by *first* name, Julie and Joy ended up next to each other.

A year ago, in fourth grade, Julie had been the new girl herself at Jack London Elementary, so she knew just how Joy felt. She was determined to help make Joy feel comfortable.

Julie glanced over at her new friend. Joy stopped fiddling with a strand of her reddish-brown hair. She leaned forward, her dark eyes intent on the teacher's face. Because Joy was deaf, she was trying to read Mrs. Duncan's lips, but she sometimes had difficulty understanding certain words. Julie knew Joy didn't like to ask questions in class—when she did, somebody always snickered at the funny-sounding way she talked.

Quietly, Julie opened the note. It said: *"A sack of wheat saved them?"*

Julie covered her mouth to stifle a giggle. She crossed out "sack of wheat" and wrote, *"Sac-a-ja-we-a, Lewis and Clark's Shoshone Indian guide."*

Julie tossed the note back to Joy just as Mrs. Duncan turned.

"Julie Albright, what have I said about passing notes?"

"Not to?" Julie asked.

"You and Miss Jenner have earned yourselves another demerit."

"But Mrs. Duncan, it's not what you think. Joy didn't understand—"

"No excuses." Mrs. Duncan pointed to the metal wastebasket. All eyes were on Julie as she trudged to the front of the room.

"Mrs. Duncan? The note's about our lesson," Julie said. "Honest. You can read it yourself."

"I don't want to argue. That's not how we do things in Room 5D."

Julie tried to explain further. "Joy was having

some trouble reading your lips."

Joy stood and pointed to herself. In her halting, too-loud tone, she stammered, "It was my fault. Not Julie's. I passed the note."

"That's enough, both of you," Mrs. Duncan snapped. "I will not take up any more class time with this nonsense. This isn't the first time I've had to speak to you about this. You will both report to detention after school. Three o'clock sharp."

Joy looked as if she'd been stung.

"But we only have two demerits," Julie protested.

"Unless you want a whole *week* of detention, you will sit down immediately. Both of you." Mrs. Duncan pursed her lips in a thin, straight line.

Joy slumped down into the hard wooden desk chair. Julie's face flushed red and she fumed all the way back to her seat. Snickers spread through the class.

"Any of you are welcome to join them in detention," Mrs. Duncan added sharply. "Now take out your silent reading. I want fifteen minutes of quiet."

Fifth grade was no fair.

❁

I will not pass notes in class.
I will not pass notes in class.
I will not pass notes in class.

Julie could not imagine writing the same sentence over and over one hundred times. Her hand hurt just thinking about it. Then she had to write *I will not talk back to the teacher* one hundred times. That sentence was even longer!

Joy sat hunched over her paper, biting her bottom lip. Julie and Joy were the only two girls at the detention table, along with several boys, including a sixth grader everybody called Stinger.

Stinger had reddish blond hair that fell over his eyes. Julie had heard the stories about him. Her friend T. J., from the basketball team, said Stinger was always picking fights on the playground and stealing kids' lunch money or tossing their bag lunches into the toilet in the boys' bathroom.

Julie rotated her wrist in circles. Her hand felt as if it were falling off and she was only on sentence number forty-nine. She picked up a magazine and leafed through it.

"Hey, no reading magazines in detention," Stinger called out, pointing.

All heads turned. Stinger got up and ambled over to Julie and Joy.

"Mr. Stenger, back to your seat. You'll recall there's also a *No talking* rule in detention," said Mr. Arnold, the vice principal. His brown mustache bristled up like a fuzzy caterpillar. "Miss Albright? Are you finished with your sentences?"

"No . . . I think I have writer's cramp. I was just giving my hand a rest for a second," Julie explained, hoping she wasn't in even more trouble.

"Back to work, everyone," said Mr. Arnold, glancing at the clock. "We still have half an hour to go."

Julie heaved a sigh and returned to her paper. She was missing shooting hoops with T. J. for this? What a waste.

Finishing her first one hundred sentences, Julie started on the next. Joy looked up and caught her eye. Julie pointed to her paper and then twirled her finger near her temple. She wondered if the sign for "cuckoo" was the same in sign language.

Joy grinned and giggled, copying Julie's "cuckoo" motion.

"Mr. Arnold, they're talking," Stinger said.

"I think I have writer's cramp. I was just giving my hand a rest for a second," Julie explained, hoping she wasn't in even more trouble.

"I didn't hear anything," said Mr. Arnold, looking up over his reading glasses.

"That's 'cause they're talking with their hands. I swear."

Mr. Arnold came over to the detention table. "Mr. Stenger, it looks to me like the girls are well ahead of you. Do you need to come up and sit next to me?"

"No, sir," said Stinger.

Julie turned back to her paper. One hour of detention felt like a week. She glanced at a poster near the window. It had a photo of a kitten clinging to a thin branch with the words *Hang in there, baby!*

Only seventy-four more lines to go.

❁

The minute detention let out, Julie was bursting to talk. Joy had to ask Julie to slow down.

"Sorry," said Julie, turning to look directly at Joy so that Joy could read her lips. "It's just that detention is such a waste!"

"I know," Joy said. "I don't see what we learned from writing the same sentence for an hour."

"We learned about writer's cramp," said Julie. Joy laughed and made a gesture as if her hand were falling off. Julie laughed, too.

A stern voice behind them said, "Detention is no laughing matter." Julie spun around and there stood Stinger, elbowing his buddies. "Gotcha. I got you so good."

Joy motioned to Julie, pointing down the street. *Let's get out of here.*

"See you tomorrow," said Stinger. "At Detention Club."

"We're not going to be in detention again tomorrow," said Julie.

"Wanna bet? Duncan Donut passes out detentions like sprinkles on donuts. She gave me forty-three detentions last year. I hold the school record," he said proudly. "Till you girls came along."

"What was that about?" Joy asked Julie as they hurried down the sidewalk.

"He thinks we're his new detention buddies," said Julie, turning to face her friend. "But I hope we never have to go back there again. Ever."

Joy held out her thumb and little finger and motioned back and forth. Julie knew this sign meant

Me, too. The girls turned the corner and headed up the hill toward their neighborhood.

"Why can't they just let us do homework in detention?" Joy asked.

"I guess that's not a punishment," said Julie. "But I don't see why we couldn't do something useful, like wash chalkboards or pick up litter on the playground."

"You should be principal," said Joy, circling the letter P over her left hand as she said the word *principal.* Julie grinned and nodded, pleased to learn a new sign. In the few weeks since school had started, Joy had taught her quite a few signs. The signs were interesting and fun to learn, like a secret code.

When the girls came to Belvedere Street, the two went separate ways, waving good-bye. Joy signed *See you later, alligator.* Julie paused, trying to remember what Joy had shown her, then signed, *After 'while, crocodile.* Joy covered her mouth, her eyes sparkling with laughter. She called, "You just said *After 'while, hippopotamus!*"

❁

As soon as Julie got home, she ran upstairs, turned on the toaster oven, and fixed herself a plate of nachos dripping with cheese. Tracy walked in and grabbed a handful.

"Hey, get your own!" said Julie.

"Shooting hoops made you hungry, huh?" Tracy asked, wiping a hand on her jeans.

Julie snorted. "No, *detention* made me hungry."

"Oh, I forgot—you're a big bad fifth grader now."

Julie made a face and scooped up another cheesy chip. "Hey, Tracy, in high school, do they make you sit and write dumb old sentences for an hour in detention?"

"How would I know?" said Tracy. "I'm not one of the *bad* kids."

"No, seriously. What do they do in high school detention?"

"Well, I think they just let you sit there and you have to be quiet. You can't talk or chew gum or eat snacks or anything, but I think you're allowed to read or do your homework, stuff like that."

"No fair," said Julie, flicking on the TV and plopping down on the sofa. Tracy squeezed in next to her.

11

"You're not getting any more nachos," Julie warned, pulling the plate onto her lap.

"So, you're watching *Little House on the Prairie*? I thought you only liked the books," Tracy taunted.

Julie moved her hand away from her face, in the direction of her sister.

"What's that supposed to mean?" Tracy asked.

"It means *bug off!*" said Julie, laughing. "It's sign language. I learned it from Joy the other day. Besides, *Little House on the Prairie* reminds me of cousin April and our big trip last summer." Julie smiled at the memory.

"I know some sign language," said Tracy.

"Really?" Julie asked, turning toward her sister with interest.

Tracy mimed putting her fingertips to her mouth. "This is the sign for *more nachos*."

Julie mimed back at her sister. "That's the sign for *ha ha, very funny*. Now, shush. Laura and Mary are coming on."

"But why isn't there any sound?" Tracy asked.

"I want to see what it would be like to have to read lips."

POSTER POWER

In civics class the next day, Mrs. Duncan was talking about elections. "It's almost time to elect a new president," she told the class. "President Ford is hoping to stay in office for the next four years, so he's running for re-election. The candidate running against him is Jimmy Carter, who used to be governor of Georgia."

"My dad's voting for Carter," said Beth.

"My dad says he's a peanut farmer!" interrupted David. "He wears sweaters like Mr. Rogers and smiles like a camel." The whole class burst out laughing.

"Interesting information, David," said Mrs. Duncan, two frown lines appearing on her brow.

Julie glanced across at Joy to see if she understood the conversation. They didn't dare pass notes in Mrs. Detention's class anymore.

"Class," said Mrs. Duncan, "your homework assignment is to read one newspaper article about Gerald Ford and one about Jimmy Carter."

Julie raised her hand. "Are we going to vote, like in an election?"

"Yes, as a matter of fact," said Mrs. Duncan. "But not for Ford or Carter," she added, flashing a rare smile. "We have school elections coming up for student body president. There will be an all-school assembly to get to know the candidates, and you'll each get to vote."

That afternoon, as Julie, Joy, and T. J. walked down the hall to their art class, Joy pointed to a new poster on the wall. It said,

> *You have a STEAK in Student Government!*
> *VOTE Salisbury for President.*

"Whoa, that's Mark Salisbury," said T. J.

"Who's he?" asked Joy.

"Only the most popular kid in sixth grade and probably the whole school," T. J. replied.

Julie frowned. "Have a *steak* in government? Give me a break. It's spelled S-T-A-K-E."

T. J. rolled his eyes. "Mellow out, Albright. What are you gonna do, give out spelling demerits?"

"Well, I'm not voting for somebody who can't spell," Julie assured him.

"It's a play on words," said T. J. "*Salisbury Steak*—don't you get it?"

Joy nodded. "I get it, but it's dumb."

"I agree," said Julie. "It's like the election is just a big joke to him. If I were student body president, I know the first thing *I'd* do."

"Give everyone spelling tests?" asked T. J.

"Ha, ha, very funny," said Julie. "No—I'd change the detention system. No more writing stupid sentences a hundred times."

"Are you nuts?" asked T. J.

"I think it's a great idea," said Joy, her hands moving with her words. "You should run for school president. I'd vote for you."

"Have you two lost your marbles? You have to be in *sixth* grade to be student body president," T. J. pointed out.

"Says who?" Julie asked.

"I don't know—it's just the rule," said T. J.

"For your information, girls weren't allowed on the boys' basketball team, and I got *that* rule changed," Julie replied.

"Well, it wouldn't matter anyway," said T. J. "You'd never beat Mark Salisbury in a million years. He practically owns the school. He's as popular as the Fonz on *Happy Days*."

In spite of her annoyance, Julie smiled. *Happy Days* was a new TV series, and her sister Tracy had a crush on the Fonz.

the Fonz

"I still think you should run," said Joy. "I'll help you."

"Hey, you could be my vice president," said Julie. "We could run together. C'mon, Joy. Let's go ask the principal.

Julie clutched the red wooden hall pass a little too tightly as she and Joy stepped into the principal's office. Crossing the sea of gold carpet again reminded her of how scared she'd been the first time she had come to talk to Mr. Sanchez—about playing on the boys' basketball team. But when he stood up from behind his large wooden desk and greeted her with a smile, she instantly relaxed.

"Miss Albright," said Mr. Sanchez. "Are you getting ready for basketball season?"

Nodding her head, Julie held up the first finger on her right hand. "I hope I don't break my finger and miss the big game this year," she said.

Mr. Sanchez smiled. "I certainly hope not. And Miss Jenner, how are you liking fifth grade at Jack London?"

"So far so good," said Joy. "I'm getting a lot better at lip reading, and Julie helps me out."

"I'm glad to see you girls are friends. Now, what brings you here today?"

Julie took a deep breath. "Well, I'm thinking of running for student body president, but somebody said you have to be in sixth grade to run. Is that true?"

Mr. Sanchez raised his eyebrows. "As far as I know, there's no rule against a fifth grader running."

"Really?" Julie said, exchanging a hopeful glance with Joy.

"It's true that the student body president has always been a sixth grader," said the principal. "But you girls have as much right to run as anyone else."

"Can we put up posters in the hall, too?" Joy asked, excitement written across her face.

"Yes, as long as you show them to Mr. Arnold first. He's in charge of student government."

"We're on our way to art class right now—maybe we can make our first poster," said Julie.

"I think this will be a good experience for you girls, and I wish you the best," said Mr. Sanchez, shaking their hands.

❖

"Mom!" Julie called, bursting through the door of Gladrags. Her mom's shop was a storefront below their second-story apartment. "Guess what! I'm going to run for school president."

Mom finished ringing up a sale, and then turned to Julie. "Hello to you, too, honey," she teased. "Take off your backpack and tell me everything."

In one breath, Julie told Mom about her exciting day. "I was wondering—can Joy come over? And is it okay to ask Ivy, too? I have to make a bunch of posters right away. The other guy already has his plastered all over the school."

"Posters sound like a great idea," said Mom. "There are plenty of art supplies in back. And you could make popcorn for a snack. I'll be up in a little while."

"Yeah, a poster party! Thanks, Mom." Julie ran upstairs to call her friends.

An hour later, Julie's living room looked like a kindergarten class. Poster boards, markers, paints, scissors, and scraps of paper littered the couch, table, and floor. The three girls sat on the rug, bent over the posters.

"You sure get to do a lot of neat stuff at your school," Ivy remarked.

"Yeah, like detention," Julie joked, and the three girls fell into a fit of giggles.

"Ivy, we thought up a bunch of slogans, but would you mind doing the rest of the lettering? Mine's all crooked. Your printing's the best," Julie said, handing her a paintbrush.

"Sure, I love doing lettering," said Ivy.

"She doesn't even have to outline in pencil first," Julie told Joy.

For the next half hour, the only sound in the room was the friendly squeaking of markers and the snip of scissors as the three girls worked.

"How do these look?" Ivy asked, holding up

a poster in each hand. *"Your future is bright with Albright,"* one poster proclaimed. *"Jump for Joy and Julie!"* said the other.

"They look great!" said Julie. She held up her own poster. "Your lettering is way better than mine."

"They look like works of art!" Joy said with admiration.

"Thanks," said Ivy, flashing a smile at Joy. "Here, now let's decorate them."

While Joy drew squiggles with glue, Julie dusted the glue with glitter.

Joy and Ivy pointed at Julie at the same time,

giggling. "You've got green glitter all over your pants," Ivy laughed.

When the girls were finished, they stood up, brushing themselves off. They lined up the posters around the room and counted.

"We have ten posters," said Ivy.

"That's twice as many as Mark has up," said Joy.

"And they look three times as good!" Julie said with satisfaction.

❧

On Thursday morning, Julie and Joy got to school early and proudly hung their posters in the hall, outside the library, and above the bleachers in the gym.

"What's all this?" asked T. J. as they were about to tape up the last poster above the fifth-grade lockers. "You can't be serious. You're really going to run for student body president against the most popular guy in the school?"

Julie and Joy exchanged a glance. "We're not afraid of that Mark guy," Joy declared.

"Besides, we have things we want to change about our school," Julie added.

"School elections aren't about changing stuff," said T. J. "They're about who's captain of the track team, or who has the most friends. It's a popularity contest. And Salisbury is *Mister* Popularity."

Julie rolled her eyes. "Are you going to stand there telling us how popular this Mark guy is, or are you going to use those hoopster arms to help us put up the last poster?"

"Okay, okay," said T. J. "Hand over the tape. But don't say I didn't warn you."

❖

At lunchtime, Julie and Joy were waiting in the cafeteria line when T. J. rushed up to them. "Quick, you guys have to see this," he said urgently. The girls left their trays and ducked under the metal railing, following T. J. to the gym, where he pointed to their posters on the wall.

Julie gasped, charging up the bleachers to take a closer look. Someone had changed the name *Joy* to *Joke*. The word *vote* now read *vomit*. And there were big black mustaches on their school pictures.

"This is so mean," said Joy, slumping down onto the bleachers.

"Who would do something like this?" asked Julie, a flash of anger darkening her eyes.

"I bet I know *exactly* who did this," said T. J.

"You saw someone?" Joy asked, pointing to her eyes and signing while she spoke.

"Well, no, but at morning recess I heard Mark tell Jeff, his vice president, what a joke it is that you're running against him."

"A joke!" Julie sputtered. "What do you mean?"

"You know, because for one thing you're a fifth grader and for another thing, well, you're a girl." T. J. looked sheepish.

Julie glared at him. "What does being a girl have to do with it?"

"I'm just telling you what I heard," said T. J., holding up both hands defensively.

"What are we going to do now?" Joy asked. "These posters are wrecked. All that work for nothing."

"We could draw mustaches on Mark, too," T. J. suggested.

"No," said Julie. "For one thing, we don't know

23

for sure if he's the one who did this. And besides, it's not right."

T. J. crossed his arms and stared hard at the posters, his eyes narrowing. "Well, whoever did this should get detention, that's for sure."

"Don't say *that*," Julie groaned. "That's what I'm trying to change." She ripped a poster down from the wall.

Joy started to pull down another poster, then stopped and looked at it thoughtfully. "We might be able to save these," she said slowly.

"How?" asked T. J. "Are you two going to grow mustaches?" He flashed a silly grin.

Joy smiled. "We can just glue new pictures on that one."

"But what about this one?" Julie asked. "It says *JOKE* in really big letters."

Joy studied the poster for a moment. "How about *Voting is no JOKE*."

"Not bad," said Julie. "I like it."

T. J. held up the poster with the word *vomit*. "I know. How about *Mark is from Planet Vomit*?"

The girls laughed. "Well, at least the other side is blank," said Julie. "Let's make a new poster right now."

"But what about lunch?" T. J. asked.

"T. J., is food all you ever think about?" Julie asked as she rolled up the poster. "C'mon, Joy, let's go."

"Wait," said T. J. "Why don't we go eat real fast and then hit the art room during recess and fix these."

The girls paused. "You mean you're going to help us?" asked Joy.

"And you're actually giving up *recess*?" Julie asked.

"Sure, why not?" said T. J. "We can't let Mark get away with this."

Julie smiled. Deep down, she knew she could count on T. J.

"I can be like the guy that runs your campaign," T. J. continued. "I'll come up with good ideas—you know, help you from behind the scenes."

"You mean like a manager?" asked Joy. "For our campaign?"

"Yep," said T. J., tearing down the last of the posters. "Campaign manager," he said slowly. "I like it. Sounds official, don't you think?"

Julie reached over and gave T. J. an exaggerated handshake. "I think you've got yourself a deal!"

CHAPTER
THREE

JULIE FOR PRESIDENT

As soon as Julie got to school on Friday morning, she made a beeline for the gym. Mr. Arnold had suggested that she and Mark each go backstage to check out the podium and test the microphone before the assembly.

Julie had never stood onstage in front of the whole school before. She'd have five minutes to talk about herself, her platform, and why she thought she would make a good student body president. Although she'd practiced the night before, just thinking about it made her stomach do a nervous, excited flip-flop.

Backstage, Julie dodged stacks of folding chairs and boxes of Drama Club props. She set her notes down on the podium and stood for a moment in the quiet dark. Closing her eyes, she imagined delivering her speech to an excited audience. Everybody hated demerits and feared detention, so she knew they would love her ideas. A shiver went up her spine—she could almost hear the clapping and cheering.

Just then, from behind the curtain, she heard voices. It sounded like the Water Fountain Girls—Angela, Amanda, and Alison, three girls from her class who were always hanging around the water fountain and talking about people in gossipy whispers.

"I can't believe he talked to us—fifth graders!" Amanda squealed.

"Where did he say to hang this poster?" Alison asked, her voice bubbling with excitement.

"Right in the center. That's where the podium will be," said Angela. "There—that looks perfect. I'm voting for him for sure."

"But what about Julie?" asked Alison. "After all, she's a fifth grader like us. Maybe we should—"

"I heard that he's going to get us a whole extra FREE DAY off from school," said Amanda.

"Sure, why not? If he can get a pool for our school, he can get a free day," Angela said confidently.

"A pool? Doesn't that cost tons of money?" asked Alison.

"Just think—we could have a swim team."

"And pool parties!" The girls squealed and giggled, jumping up and down.

"I feel kind of bad for Julie, though," said Alison. "She doesn't stand a chance."

"She might have half a chance if it weren't for that deaf girl running with her," Amanda said. "I mean, what was she thinking?"

Julie caught her breath, and her face turned hot. Just then, she heard footsteps behind her. *Joy*. Julie turned and put a finger to her lips, motioning for Joy to be quiet.

"Yeah, no one in their right mind's going to vote for her," said Angela. "She's always staring and waving her hands around like this." There was a pause, and the other two girls cackled. "And she sounds so weird when she talks."

"I know," Amanda agreed. "If Julie wants to get any votes at all, she better dump that deaf girl before the assembly. Once she opens her mouth, it's all over."

Julie's forehead felt as if it were on fire. She

Julie turned and put a finger to her lips, motioning for Joy to be quiet.

hoped it was too dark backstage for Joy to see her burning face.

"We'd better get to class," said Alison. "The bell's about to ring."

When Julie was sure the girls were gone, she burst through the curtain and jumped down off the stage to get a look at the poster they'd hung. Joy followed close behind. Julie couldn't look at her.

"What's wrong?" Joy asked. Her too-loud voice seemed to echo in the empty gym.

"Nothing," said Julie.

"It's those girls, isn't it?" Joy came close and touched Julie's hand. "Did they say something mean about you?"

Julie took a deep breath to calm herself. She couldn't bring herself to tell Joy they were saying mean things about *her*. But Joy read it in her face.

"Oh, I get it. They were talking about me, weren't they?" Joy asked. She was turning angry now—her hands flew in the air, signing forcefully along with each spoken word.

Clearing her throat, Julie tried to look casual. "Don't worry about them. They were just saying that we—we don't stand a chance against Mark."

"I know they don't like me," Joy said flatly. "It's because I'm deaf, isn't it?"

Julie turned to her friend, looking her straight in the eye. "I know it must be hard not being able to hear. But trust me, some things are better off not being heard."

❖

No sooner was Julie back in class than she looked at her empty hands and realized she didn't have her note cards. In a panic, she tapped Joy and asked, "Did you see my note cards? Was I holding them when you came backstage?"

"No," Joy shook her head. "I didn't see them."

"I must have left them on the podium. I was going to practice, but then—" Julie paused, thinking. "Tell Mrs. Duncan I'll be back in a minute."

"But you'll be late—" Joy protested, pointing to the clock as Julie zoomed off down the hall.

Julie walked as fast as she could without running on her way to the gym. It was all she could do not to sprint. One thing she did not need was another demerit for running in the halls.

Rushing up the back steps onto the stage, she

marched straight to the podium, but her note cards were nowhere to be seen. She looked all around the podium and on the floor around the stage, but it was no use. Her note cards were gone.

❖

Mrs. Duncan tried to get the class to focus on Lewis and Clark, but the students were buzzing with excitement about the assembly. Julie sat silently, trying not to panic and wondering how she would give a speech without her notes. It was almost a relief when an announcement came over the loudspeaker and Mrs. Duncan told the class to line up by rows at the door.

On the way to the gym, Julie whispered to Joy, "What am I going to do?"

You've practiced that speech a million times. You know it by heart. You'll do great, Joy signed silently. Julie nodded to show Joy she understood, and smiled gratefully.

As the students took their seats, Mr. Arnold tapped the microphone. "Testing. Testing. Welcome, students, to the official kickoff of the 1976 election for student body president. As most of you know, this

November our country will be electing a new president of the United States. And we here at Jack London Elementary are electing a new school president. Today, we'll get a chance to hear from the candidates. First up will be sixth grader Mark Salisbury."

The audience went wild. Sixth graders stomped their feet, rattling the bleachers and yelling, "Go, Mark! Yahoo!"

Mark stepped up to the podium. He took out his note cards, tapped them on the podium, and cleared his throat.

"Fellow students, I know you don't want to listen to a long boring speech with lots of promises, so I promise to make this short and sweet. One word will sum up my platform." He leaned in toward the microphone. "Pizza!"

The audience clapped and cheered.

"If I am elected president," Mark went on, "I promise to get pizza every Friday for hot lunch in the cafeteria. No more mystery meat and stewed tomatoes." Then Mark clapped his hands together and started a chant, "Piz-za Fri-day, Piz-za Fri-day," and soon he had nearly all the students clapping and chanting. Mark stepped away from the podium and took several dramatic bows, hamming it up for the audience.

Pizza? That's why he's running for school president? Julie thought to herself, but she looked out at the other students and saw that they were completely swept up in the moment. Her stomach did a nervous cartwheel. All of a sudden, the speech she had prepared seemed much too serious. Maybe she should just scrap the whole thing and think up a catchy word or gimmick, as Mark had. But it was too late. Mark was already passing her on the stage, taking his seat.

"Forget your note cards, Albright?" Mark said under his breath. So Mark must have found her note cards after she checked the podium, and taken them! T. J. was right—Mark really was a sleazeball. She couldn't just let him win. Julie sat with her hands clenched in her lap, hoping to steady herself as Mr. Arnold introduced her.

". . . and we thought Mark was going to run un-opposed, but fifth grader Julie Albright has decided to make this a real contest. So let's give a warm welcome to Julie Albright."

Several students clapped politely, but there were

no hoots or hollers as there had been for Mark. A hiss of "fifth grader" went through the sixth-grade bleachers.

Julie longed for her note cards, just to have something to hold on to. As she stepped up to the podium, she reminded herself why she was running—because of something she believed in. Because she wanted to make her school a better place.

"Principals, teachers, and fellow students," Julie began, suddenly thinking of a good way to start her speech. "I like pizza as much as anybody, but today I'm here to talk to you about something that affects us all—detention."

"Bor-ing," a boy in the back row called out.

Swallowing hard, Julie plunged ahead. She briefly outlined her plan to do away with detention and demerits.

The gymnasium grew dead quiet. Students looked sideways at teachers, not sure how to react, as though they might get in trouble for just thinking about the idea. Then a group of sixth-grade boys, led by Stinger, began hooting and stomping at the top of the bleachers. Stinger started his own chant, "Down with detention!

Down with detention!" but it quickly fizzled out.

Julie nervously brushed back her hair, shifting from foot to foot. "What I mean to say is, instead of sitting in detention writing sentences over and over, we could be doing something positive for our school." She looked out at the audience. Hundreds of eyes stared blankly at her.

She raised her voice a notch. "Um, we could scrub graffiti off the bathroom walls. Or plant flowers, or pick up litter—stuff like that." Still no reaction. The bright spotlight glared down on her. Julie wiped beads of sweat from her forehead. She couldn't for the life of her remember how her speech ended. Hurriedly thanking the audience, she sat down. A few weak claps here and there seemed to mock her.

Mr. Arnold thanked her and made some final remarks. Julie didn't hear them. She fixed her eyes on the plaid pattern of his shirt and willed herself not to cry.

❧

When Julie got home from school that day, she dragged herself into the apartment, dropped her backpack, and slumped onto the couch.

"How did your speech go today, honey?" Mom asked, exchanging glances with Tracy.

"Not too good, from the looks of it," said Tracy as she headed into the kitchen for a snack.

Mom put down her laundry basket and sat next to Julie on the couch. "Tell me about it, honey."

"It was a disaster." Julie explained about her missing note cards, Mark and his Pizza Fridays, and the silent reaction she'd gotten to her ideas. "The bad kids were the only ones who liked it!"

"You still have more than a week to go before the election," said Mom. "Anything can happen in politics. Look at Jimmy Carter. Everybody loved him after the Democratic convention this summer, and they were upset with Ford because he pardoned Nixon after Watergate."

"But I thought Nixon lied," said Julie.

"That's why a lot of people started looking at Carter. Then Carter announced that he would pardon all the Vietnam War draft dodgers—those young men who left the country rather than fight in a war they didn't believe in," Mom explained. "Now it's a much closer race."

Tracy poked her head out of the kitchen doorway.

"My civics teacher said he admires Carter for having the courage to say what he believes is right, even though it's unpopular."

"See?" said Mom. "Carter may lose votes over his ideas, but he'll gain some, too. Look at Hank. He told me he's voting for Carter because he thinks the war was wrong, and he's a Vietnam veteran."

"Who are you going to vote for, Mom?" Julie asked.

"I'm going to vote for Jimmy Carter," Mom told her. "I like his ideas, and I think this country needs a change."

Julie nodded. "That's what I'm trying to do for our school—make a change."

But even as she said the words, Julie knew it wouldn't be as simple as she had thought. She remembered last year when she had tried to join the boys' basketball team. "Any time you try to change something, it's going to be difficult," her mom had warned, and she had been right.

Change had been hard to accept in her own life after her parents' divorce. It had taken time to get used to, and she'd had to find a new way of thinking about her family. Julie realized that if she wanted people to be open to her ideas, she would have to give them a new way to look at detention—a new way of thinking about it. But how?

Mom handed Julie a pile of folded laundry. "Here, honey—some clean clothes if you want to take them to Dad's this weekend. You'd better get packed. He'll be here any minute."

❧

That evening after dinner, while Julie helped Dad with the dishes, she asked, "Dad, are you going to vote for Carter or Ford for president?"

"Well, I'll tell you, I've been thinking a lot about this," Dad said, looking up from scraping the bottom of the pot roast pan. "Right now, I'm planning to vote for President Ford."

"But what about Carter?"

"Carter seems like a decent man, but we just don't know much about him," Dad answered. "And I'm not sure this country is ready for some of his new ideas. Americans have been through a lot in the past few years. I think it might be better to stick with a familiar president who knows how to run the country."

Julie dried off a dinner plate and stacked it in the

cupboard. "Do you think you might change your
mind?" she asked him.

"Well, so far there's been only one debate on TV,
and I think Ford came out ahead on that one. But
there's another debate next week, right here in
San Francisco in fact, and I'll be watching it to hear
what both candidates have to say."

Julie stopped drying the bowl in her hand. "How
come the debates are so important?"

"In a debate, you get a much better idea of what
the candidates think on all kinds of issues," Dad
explained, handing the pot roast pan over to Julie.
"Tell you what—if you're interested, I'll come pick
you up and we can watch the debates together."

"Really? That would be groovy," said Julie,
feeling very grown-up. Tracy and her teenage friends
often said *groovy*. Julie finished drying the pan and
hung up her damp towel. "And you know what,
Dad? This just gave me a great idea for my campaign."

HEATING UP

On Monday morning, Julie and Mark had a meeting with Mr. Arnold. Julie suggested a debate between the candidates.

"I think that's a great idea, Julie," said the vice principal. But Mark looked shocked.

"You want me to debate a *girl*?" Mark said, as if Julie weren't even in the room. He put his hands on his hips. "Is there any rule that says I have to?"

"There's no rule," said Mr. Arnold. "But it would be a great opportunity for the students to get to know the candidates better."

"They already know *me*," said Mark.

"All they know is that you want pizza for school lunch," said Julie. "This would give us a chance to debate other issues we care about."

Mark wouldn't look at Julie. "Why should I help her?" he asked Mr. Arnold. "She already knows she's going to lose."

"I'm sorry you see it that way, Mark," said Mr. Arnold. "I think a debate would be a terrific experience. I'd like you to think it over."

"Sorry," said Mark, turning to go. "Not interested."

❖

As Julie headed down the hall toward her locker, she felt disappointment dragging her steps. Earlier that morning, she'd jumped out of bed, excited about the possibility of a debate. But Mark had burst her bubble, and she was back to feeling helpless and frustrated.

"You look like we just lost a basketball game or something," said T. J. He and Joy were standing near Julie's locker, waiting for her.

As they headed to class, Julie started to tell her friends about the debate.

"Whoa," said T. J., his face lighting up. "That's a great idea."

"You're brave," said Joy. "It would be hard to get up in front of all those people again and debate Mark."

"Doesn't matter," Julie sighed. "Mark said no."

T. J. stopped in his tracks. "What do you mean he said no?"

Julie shrugged. "He knows he's going to win, so why should he debate me?"

"If he's so sure, then why's he afraid to debate you?" T. J. asked.

"He doesn't want to, and he doesn't have to," said Julie.

"We just have to think up another way to get our ideas across," said Joy.

"Maybe this'll help," said T. J. He reached into his backpack and pulled out two buttons that said *NO DETENTION*.

"You made these?" asked Joy. "For us?"

"My dad has a button-making machine," said T. J. "I was thinking you guys could wear these. You'll be like walking ads. Maybe it'll help get your ideas out."

"Wow," said Julie, pinning her button to her sweater. "Thanks, T. J."

"Hey, what are campaign managers for?" He

43

bobbed his head, a hunk of sandy hair flopping over his eyes, and smiled ear to ear.

"I have an idea," said Joy. "Maybe we could stand by the front door after school and talk to kids as they get on their buses. We can wear our buttons and tell them about changing the detention system."

"Brilliant," Julie said, grinning.

❖

When the day was over and the final bell rang, Julie and Joy headed down to the front lobby. Kids started pouring down the halls and out the front door.

"No more detention," Julie called out as kids filed past her. "Vote for Julie. Change the system."

Kids hurried past her, eager to get to their buses. *Nobody's even listening,* thought Julie. She peeled one of their posters off the wall and turned to Joy. "Here, hold this poster out so all the kids will see it, while I do the talking."

Julie went up to a group of kids and asked them what they thought about demerits and detention. The students stared silently at her. Nervously, she glanced at Joy. Joy stood stiffly, barely holding up the poster.

A boy in a red jacket bumped into Joy and gave her an unfriendly look. "Hey, watch out. You're blocking the way."

"Joy," said Julie impatiently, "why are you just standing there? Can't you hold up the poster like I said?"

Joy let the poster drop. As she spoke, her hands flew so fast, Julie had to step back to get out of the way. *I may be deaf, but I can still speak for myself.*

"Sorry," said Julie. "I didn't mean—never mind. Don't worry about the poster. Let's both talk to as many kids as we can. There's not much time before the buses leave."

Joy stood by the other set of doors. "Hi, I'm Joy Jenner," she started, but Julie watched the kids brush right past her. "Vote for Julie for school president," Joy tried again. The kids began heading out the opposite door to avoid walking past her.

"Who is that girl, anyway?" asked a girl in a corduroy jumper.

"When she talks, she sounds like she's inside a fishbowl," said another.

"Maybe her name's Flipper!" said a boy, and he began singing the *Flipper* theme song all the way to the bus. *"They call her Flipper, Flipper, faster than lightning . . ."*

Julie crumpled inside. She had known that the other kids thought Joy was weird, strange, different. What she hadn't realized—until now, seeing it with her own eyes—was that this made them a little bit afraid of her.

Watching the kids skirt around Joy to the other exit, Julie suddenly felt dizzy with uncertainty. She knew it wouldn't be right to ask Joy not to speak up for herself. But Julie had to admit that when Joy did speak, it made things worse. The truth was, having Joy for a vice president was ruining any chance she had at being elected student body president—or even at getting kids to think about her ideas. But how on earth could she tell her friend that?

When the final bus pulled away from the curb, Julie couldn't help feeling relieved. The girls began walking home in silence.

"Want to come walk the dogs with me today?" Joy finally asked when they got to Belvedere Street.

"I—I can't, not today. Sorry," Julie stammered. Feeling guilty, she rushed off toward home.

❖

Julie dropped her backpack inside the front door and went straight to her room, fighting back tears. A few minutes later, she heard Tracy yell, "Hey, why'd you dump your stuff in the middle of the doorway? I almost tripped and broke my—" But when Tracy got to Julie's room and saw her sister's face, she stopped.

"Jules?" she asked softly. "Are you okay?"

Julie didn't answer. Tracy sat down on the bed next to her. "Did something happen at school? Do you want to talk about it?"

"It's the election," Julie said dully. "Nobody gets my ideas, and Mark, the guy I'm running against, won't even be in a debate with me. Then today, when Joy and I tried to talk to kids about our ideas, everybody acted like we had major cooties."

"Cooties?" Tracy asked, trying to hold back a little smile.

"It's not funny!" said Julie. "It's like they think Joy has a disease and they're afraid they'll catch it. They look at her like she's weird. They call her names and say awful stuff about her, and she can't even hear them."

47

"I know—kids can be so mean," said Tracy. "In high school, some people are mean if they think you wear the wrong clothes." She reached over and smoothed out the bedspread between them.

"It's all a huge mess," Julie moaned. "I hate to say it, but I even started thinking maybe I should ask T. J. to run with me instead. I don't have a chance of winning with Joy as my vice president. Of course, I probably wouldn't win anyway. And I don't want to lose her as a friend." With a groan, Julie fell back on her bed. "Why did I ever think running for student body president was a good idea? It's the worst idea I've ever had."

❖

The next morning, when Julie and Joy passed through the front doors of the school, they stopped, stunned.

Mark and Jeff stood at the front door, shaking hands with kids as they poured off the buses and headed for their classrooms. "I'm Mark Salisbury, your next student body president," Mark said, smiling with a big, toothy grin.

"He stole our idea!" said Joy.

Julie nodded but didn't say a word.

At their lockers, Julie turned to Joy. "We might as well admit it—Mark has us beat. He's going to win by a landslide. Let's just drop out of the race now and not give that Pizza Monster the satisfaction of eating us alive." Julie forced herself to meet Joy's eyes.

Joy looked surprised. She searched Julie's face. "That's not like you to quit," Joy said finally.

"I know, but—well, nothing has turned out the way I expected. It just seems like dropping out is the best thing to do now." *Please don't make this harder than it already is,* Julie begged silently.

"It's me, isn't it?" Joy looked at the floor. "I may be deaf, but I'm not blind. Nobody likes me. I'm the one they avoid. They don't even give you a chance because of me."

Julie buried her head in her locker so that Joy wouldn't see the truth of it on her face.

"If anybody drops out, it should be me," Joy went on. "You can ask T. J. to be your vice president. He's on the basketball team with you, and everybody likes him. But most of all, he's not deaf."

Julie wanted to protest, but instead she heard

herself mumble, "Um, the bell's about to ring. We'd better get to class."

✿

Mrs. Duncan called on her twice that morning, and Julie fumbled through her notebook to find the right answers. She willed herself to sit up and pay attention to Lewis and Clark's ongoing journey. And Julie had to admit it *was* a pretty exciting journey. They had faced wild bears and raging rivers and long months of hardship. It reminded Julie of her wagon train trip last summer for the Bicentennial, although she knew Lewis and Clark's journey had been a lot more dangerous.

"'Courage undaunted, possessing a firmness and perseverance of purpose,'" said Mrs. Duncan. "That's how Thomas Jefferson described Lewis. What did he mean by that?"

The students squirmed in their seats, looking blankly back at the teacher. Slowly, one hand rose.

"Joy?" said Mrs. Duncan.

"I think he meant that Lewis was brave," Joy said slowly in her odd voice, "and that he didn't give up." She glanced sideways at Julie.

Julie blinked in surprise. Joy almost never spoke up in class. Was her friend trying to send her a message?

❧

At lunch, T. J. practically tripped over himself racing up to Julie and Joy. "You're not going to believe this," he said, cutting in line next to them. "Did you see the signs I put up this morning that say 'Where's the Debate?' Everybody's buzzing about it—and now they want a debate."

"What?" Joy asked.

"Are you serious?" Julie asked.

T. J. nodded. "Get this—Jeff, Mark's own vice president, asked him why he's afraid to debate a girl. And guess what? Mark didn't know what to say, so he finally agreed to do it. You got your debate!"

"Too bad somebody's dropping out of the election," said Joy.

"What? Who—you?" T. J. asked, looking from Joy to Julie.

"I didn't say it was for sure," said Julie defensively. She couldn't admit that she'd been thinking about letting Joy drop out.

"You can't quit now," said T. J. "The election's just heating up!"

T. J. and Joy were right—she couldn't quit now. Julie firmly grasped her lunch tray and tossed back her hair, as if to shake off any lingering doubts about running with Joy or dropping out of the race.

❖

"D-Day," T. J. said, coming up to Julie in the hall on Thursday morning.

"Huh?" Julie turned and gave him a blank look.

"Debate Day." He elbowed her in the ribs good-naturedly.

Julie bit her bottom lip. Now that the debate was here, her stomach fluttered with nervous anticipation. But she reminded herself that this was the best way to get her ideas across, and that steadied her.

When it was time for the debate, Julie took her place onstage at a podium opposite Mark. She stood squinting in the bright spotlight, looking out over the rows of students until she spotted Joy and T. J. in the audience. He had told her it might help to fix her eyes on a friendly face or two at first.

Mr. Arnold gave a short introduction, explaining

the ground rules and time limits of the debate. He would ask a question, and each candidate would have a turn to answer. "Please hold your applause until the very end," said Mr. Arnold. "Now, first question: Why is student government important? Miss Albright, we'll begin with you."

Leaning in to the microphone, Julie said, "Student government is important because it gives all of us a say in what happens at our school."

"Mr. Salisbury?"

"Student government is important because we get to plan fun activities, like going to Marine World."

The crowd clapped and cheered, and Mr. Arnold had to remind them to hold their applause.

"Julie," said Mr. Arnold, glancing at his index cards, "Mark has proposed Pizza Fridays as his platform. Tell us what you think of his idea."

"Pizza's great!" said Julie. "I just think there are more important things to work on, like changing the detention system."

"Thank you, Julie. Mr. Salisbury, your comments on Julie's idea to change the detention system?"

"She doesn't know what she's talking about," said Mark.

"Pizza's great!" said Julie. "I just think there are more important things, like changing the detention system."

"Yes I do," said Julie. "I've *been* to detention." The crowd laughed. "That's how I know we need to change it."

"Julie, I'm going to have to ask you to wait your turn to speak," Mr. Arnold cautioned.

"Sorry," said Julie, blushing and stepping away from the podium.

"If we didn't have detention," said Mark, "then all the bullies could do whatever they wanted, and the bad kids would take over the school. Everybody knows that. Or at least by the time you get to sixth grade, you do. Think about it—do you really want a student body president and vice president who have both been in detention?"

"Mr. Arnold," said Julie, raising her hand. "May I say one more thing?"

Mr. Arnold looked at his watch. "I'll allow a rebuttal. You have one minute."

Julie took a deep breath. The audience was silent, watching. And listening. "Of course if a student does something wrong, there has to be a consequence," she began. "But I don't see how sitting in detention and writing a sentence over and over a hundred times helps anybody. What I am saying is if we break

55

a rule, we should make up for it by doing something good, instead of something useless that just gives you writer's cramp."

"Your one minute is up," said Mr. Arnold. "Mark, you have one minute to reply."

"Detention isn't supposed to be fun," said Mark. "It's supposed to be a punishment."

"But we should learn from our mistakes," said Julie. "And I think we'd learn more if we did something useful. Something that helps the whole school."

To Julie's surprise, the students burst into applause. Mr. Arnold had to quiet them down once more.

"Okay, let's move on," said Mr. Arnold. "Final question: If for some reason you had to leave the office of student body president, your vice president would take your place. Please tell us what qualifies him or her for this position. Mark?"

"Easy," said Mark. "My VP, Jeff Coopersmith, is captain of the crossing guards. Everybody knows him, and he's real tall so it would be easy to find him when you need him." Everyone laughed.

"Thank you, Mark. Julie, can you tell us what qualifies your vice president to hold the office of student body president?"

Julie froze. The whole audience seemed to hold its breath, and for one long, awkward moment, all eyes were on Julie, waiting.

In the vast quiet, Julie heard herself begin to talk. "My vice president, Joy Jenner, is new to our school. Because she's new, many of you haven't gotten to know her. Instead of speaking for her, I'd like to ask her to come up to the podium and speak for herself."

In utter silence, all heads turned to watch Joy as she walked down the center aisle and up onto the stage. Julie stepped back from the microphone. Joy gripped the sides of the podium, as if steadying herself in a strong wind. Her eyelids fluttered and she took in a deep breath. When she opened her mouth, nothing came out.

Julie reached over and gave Joy's hand a soft squeeze. The whole audience seemed to sit closer, leaning in to hear Joy's words.

"I know I'm different," Joy started. "I know I talk funny. I can't hear what you hear because I'm deaf. But everybody feels different sometimes. And even though I'm deaf, I promise to listen to you. I hope you'll give me a chance."

Wow! Great job, Julie signed to Joy while Mr. Arnold thanked everyone and wrapped up the assembly.

Wow!

As Julie's class headed down the hall to their classroom, Mrs. Duncan lingered to congratulate the girls. "Julie, you did us proud in Room 5D." Julie beamed at the rare praise from her teacher. Then Mrs. Duncan turned to Joy. "Joy, I know it was difficult for you to speak in front of the whole school, but you really shined."

"Thanks," said Joy. She touched a hand to her chin, signing *thank you* with a shy smile.

As they approached their classroom, Julie heard a commotion inside. Through the open door, she could see the Water Fountain Girls standing in front of the whole class. Alison was holding out a bottle of glue like a microphone, and Amanda was speaking into it using a loud, nasal voice to imitate Joy at the podium during the debate. Angela was flailing her arms about in mock sign language.

"What in the world!" Mrs. Duncan barked. The three girls turned, red-faced. Marching into the classroom, Mrs. Duncan blinked the lights on and off, clapping sharply to get the class settled down.

"Class! That is e-nough," she said, each syllable as sharp as her clapping. "At this school, we respect others, despite our differences."

In horror, Julie glanced at Joy. Joy's face twisted with pain, and she rushed off down the hall. "Joy, wait up," Julie called, hurrying after her. But her words just echoed down the empty corridor, unheard.

Julie found Joy crumpled on the floor in a corner of the girls' bathroom. She knelt beside her on the cold tile and gently put a hand on Joy's shoulder.

Finally, Joy raised her tear-stained face. "I did my best, but it wasn't enough. They think I'm stupid—stupid like a clown." She put her head in her arms and sobbed.

Julie swallowed, feeling her eyes well with sympathy. She didn't know what she could say to help Joy feel better. Finally, she tapped Joy on the shoulder to get her attention. "Last year, when I was the new girl, those same girls said mean stuff about me, too. I know how you feel." But even as Julie spoke the words, she wasn't so sure. It was one thing to have the Water Fountain Girls talk about you behind your back in the halls or at the water fountain. It was another thing for them to make fun of someone in front of the whole class.

Joy shook her head and looked away. "I can't go back there, ever."

"Joy, listen—you can't hide in the girls' bathroom forever. Pretty soon the lunch bell will ring and there'll be a ton of kids in here."

Joy pulled herself up. "I don't feel so good," she said, clutching her knees.

Julie put her arm around Joy. "C'mon, I'll walk you to the nurse's office."

❁

When Julie got back to class, Mrs. Duncan stepped out into the hall with her. "Where's Joy? Is she all right?"

Julie shook her head. "She has a stomach ache, so she's lying down in the nurse's office."

Mrs. Duncan rubbed her forehead. "I'll check on her later. Let's give her some time to herself. It was terribly hurtful what those girls did. They will have to apologize to Joy."

Julie nodded and headed back to her seat. She flushed as she felt eyes on her, and she stared straight ahead at her desk to avoid making eye contact with the Water Fountain Girls. The empty desk beside her seemed to announce its presence. Julie tried to concentrate on her math worksheet, but none of the columns seemed to add up.

❧

Julie stared at the Sloppy Joe on her lunch tray. She hadn't touched a bite of her food.

T. J. plopped his tray down next to Julie's. "Boy oh boy, I've never seen Duncan Donut so mad. When you and Joy were gone, she really blasted those girls. You should have seen it. She was practically spitting when she gave them detention."

Julie looked up from her tray. "They got detention?"

"More like triple detention. They have to write 'I will not make fun of others' three hundred times. That's like six pages front and back!"

"Oh, no." Julie put her head in her hands.

"What!? They deserve it!" T. J. said heatedly. "You guys were boss in that debate. You beat the pants off Mark, and all they did was make fun of

61

you." He took a big bite of his Sloppy Joe.

"That's not the point, T. J.," Julie moaned.

"Listen, Julie," T. J. said with his mouth full. "I know you're against detention, but this time they really deserve it."

Julie hated to admit it, but part of her just wanted to see the Water Fountain Girls punished.

T. J. leaned across the table toward her. "Are you saying they should get away with it?"

Julie shook her head. It was starting to ache. She took a sip of her chocolate milk.

"Well?" T. J. asked, still waiting for an answer.

"T. J., if those girls do a dumb detention where they write the same sentence a million times, how will that help anything? Will it make them sorry for what they did? You know it won't—it'll just make them hate Joy more than ever. After all, if it wasn't for her, they wouldn't be stuck in detention in the first place. That's how they'll see it."

"I guess," T. J. shrugged. "That's just how kids are."

"And that's why detention doesn't work."

"Well, okay then, Miss Smartypants—if you were Mrs. Duncan, what would *you* do?"

Julie rubbed her forehead. "I'm not sure."

"Good thing it's not up to you, then," said T. J. "Hey, can I have your Sloppy Joe if you're not going to eat it?"

Julie pushed it toward him. "Here." She got up. "I'm going to see how Joy's doing."

But when she got to the nurse's office, the cot was empty, and the nurse told Julie that Joy had gone home.

THE ELECTION

That afternoon, Julie was grateful that her class made a trip to the library. Even though she missed giggling in the corner with Joy, it gave her some quiet time to think.

Her thoughts were in a tangle. As much as she wanted to see the Water Fountain Girls pay for what they'd done, she knew in her heart that detention wasn't the answer. Writing sentences wouldn't change the Water Fountain Girls at all, or make school better for Joy.

But what *was* the answer?

Julie fiddled with the macramé key chain on the end of her house key, twisting and untwisting the knots and loose ends. Over and over in her head she heard T. J.'s words—*If you were Mrs. Duncan, what would you do?*

Julie looked around the library, groping for an idea. Her eyes landed on the familiar Dewey Decimal poster, the beanbag pillow on the floor of the story corner, the stuffed animals lining the tops of the low shelves. She scanned the spines of the books against the back wall. Biographies. *Anne Frank: The Diary of a Young Girl. And Then What Happened, Paul Revere?* She stared at the shelves directly in front of her. The 400s. Languages. *How to Speak Spanish.*

Languages. It was as if Joy spoke a foreign language, one that the Water Fountain Girls did not understand.

But what if they could speak her language? Maybe if they got to know Joy, they wouldn't act so mean and cruel.

"Last call for checking out books," called Mrs. Paterson, the librarian, startling Julie out of her deep thought.

Julie hopped up. There *was* a book she wanted to check out, if she could find the right one. Running her fingers along the spines, she saw it: *Sign Language Is Fun.* She took it to the checkout desk.

"Going to learn some sign language, Julie?" asked Mrs. Paterson.

"You know my friend Joy Jenner?" Julie asked. "She already taught me some signs, but I want to learn some new signs to surprise her."

"Good for you," said Mrs. Paterson, stamping the date due card and sliding it back into the pocket.

As Julie headed back to class, she flipped through the book thoughtfully. *Poster. President. School.* This book had all the signs she would need.

Suddenly, she knew how to answer T. J.'s question. Now she just had to get Mrs. Duncan to go along with her idea.

❖

The final bell rang. While the other students hurriedly gathered their books and clunked their chairs upside-down on their desks, the Water Fountain Girls dragged themselves out the door and off to detention.

"Mrs. Duncan?" Julie asked, hugging her books to her chest as she approached the teacher's desk. "May I ask you a question?"

"What is it, Julie?" Mrs. Duncan sounded tired.

66

"Mrs. Duncan," Julie repeated, "I know what those girls did was wrong, and they hurt Joy a lot. But I've been thinking—um, well, how is writing sentences going to help them to learn from what they did or make them act better in the future?"

"I'm not sure what you're suggesting, Julie. I know you have a low opinion of detention, but it will force those girls to write and think about what they've done."

"Will it?" asked Julie. "Just look at Stinger—detention doesn't seem to be making *him* act any better. Last year, you gave him forty-three detentions, and he hasn't changed one bit."

"Well, I'll give you that," said Mrs. Duncan, gathering up the folders on her desk and sliding them into her tote bag. "All right, Julie. Go ahead—tell me what you're thinking."

Julie held up her library book for Mrs. Duncan to see. "I was thinking I could teach them some sign language."

Mrs. Duncan's eyes widened with surprise, but Julie kept right on talking. "Joy taught me lots of signs, and I'm learning even more from this book. Maybe if they learned some sign language, it would help them understand Joy a little better, and they

67

wouldn't feel like she's so weird or different anymore . . . " Julie stopped twisting the hem of her shirt and looked anxiously at Mrs. Duncan. Was her teacher angry with her?

Mrs. Duncan was quiet. She shuffled some papers on her desk. She picked up her calendar book and put it in her bag. Julie felt certain that the creases in her teacher's forehead were disapproving.

After what felt like forever, Mrs. Duncan set down her tote bag. She looked up at Julie and said, "You know what? Maybe this is worth a try." She scribbled out a note and handed it to Julie. "Go on down to the library and give this note to Mr. Arnold. Ask the girls to come back to the classroom. I can stay an extra hour today."

"Really? You mean it?" Julie let out a breath. "Thank you, Mrs. Duncan."

"No, thank you," said Mrs. Duncan. "After twenty-three years of teaching, I just might be learning something new."

❧

The Water Fountain Girls were leery as they followed Julie back to the classroom.

"What did you pull us out of detention for?" Angela huffed.

"We weren't even half done writing our sentences. You better not be getting us in more trouble," said Amanda.

"You want to go back there?" Julie snapped. "Go right ahead—be my guest. Excuse me for thinking maybe you'd rather do something besides write a million sentences till your hands fall off. Not that you don't deserve it."

"What do you mean?" Alison asked.

"Are you saying you're going to get us out of writing all those sentences?" asked Angela. "Why would you be nice to us? What's the catch?"

Julie glared at her. "All you think about are yourselves. Did you ever stop to think for one minute about Joy—that I might be doing something for *her*, not for you?"

As Julie explained her idea, Angela rolled her eyes and Amanda stood with her hand on her hip. Alison just stared at the floor. When Julie was finished, there was a long, uncomfortable silence.

Finally Alison looked up at her friends. "Well, at least this sounds better than detention."

"I guess," said Amanda reluctantly.

"It's not like we really have a choice," Angela muttered as they followed Julie into Mrs. Duncan's room.

Alison, Amanda, and Angela pulled their chairs to form a semicircle around Julie. She started out by helping each girl create a unique sign for her name. Then she showed them a few simple signs, like *hello* and *please*. Next, Julie looked up signs in her library book for things around the room—clock, window, desk, globe, hamster—and showed them how to make the hand signs.

hello

please

"This is hard," Angela grumbled. "I can't make my fingers work right."

"I'll teach you how to finger-spell," Julie said. Soon she, Alison, Amanda, and Angela were singing "*A-B-C-D-E-F-G*," moving their hands in time to the song and trying to remember the finger positions for each letter. They ran through the song a few times, faster and faster, and ended breathless and laughing.

"I never in a million years thought I'd be singing the alphabet song in fifth grade!" Alison exclaimed.

"My fingers are all tangled up," Amanda said with a giggle.

Even Angela cracked a small smile.

"Girls, I'm afraid that's all the time we have for today," said Mrs. Duncan.

The four girls were quiet as they put their chairs back up onto the desks and gathered their books and belongings.

Alison leaned on the rungs of her upside-down chair for a moment and breathed a heavy sigh. "Julie?" she started softly. "Does this mean you're not mad at us?"

Julie hesitated for a moment. Then she rubbed her thumb against her index finger.

"What does that mean?" Alison asked.

"A little bit," Julie said.

Alison looked grateful and gave her a quick smile.

Amanda had edged closer. Suddenly she blurted out, "Do you think Joy will ever forgive us for what we did?"

"I don't know," Julie answered.

Alison spoke up again. "Before we go, will you show us how to sign the word *sorry*?"

"Okay, sure," said Julie. "First, make the letter *A*." She held out a fist with her thumb facing up. "Then rub it in a circle over your heart."

sorry

All three girls watched Julie intently. Then, carefully, they formed their hands into the letter *A* and made circles over their hearts.

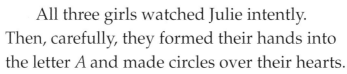

On Friday morning, when Julie arrived at school, Amanda, Alison, and Angela were waiting inside the front lobby. They rushed up to her.

"Where's Joy?" Angela demanded.

"She's coming today, right?" asked Amanda.

Julie shook her head. "I stopped by her house on the way to school, but her mother said she still isn't feeling well."

"But it's Friday—that means we won't see her until Monday," said Alison, looking distressed.

The three girls exchanged a glance.

"We can't wait till Monday," said Angela. "We have to tell her we're sorry."

"We *want* to tell her," Alison added.

Julie shifted her backpack, thinking.

72

"Hey, Julie," said Amanda, "do you think we could have detention again today?"

"Huh?" Julie asked. "You mean—"

"Yeah, you know, stay after school, like yesterday, and learn more signs," Amanda explained.

Julie looked up, startled, and then broke into a grin. "Oh, so you think my idea for changing detention is better than Pizza Fridays?"

The three girls looked sheepish at first. Then Angela looked up. "Well, duh!" she said, and all four girls laughed.

"Tell you what," said Julie. "Why don't we hold detention at Joy's house after school today. Maybe we can cheer her up."

❀

After school, the four girls walked to Joy's house. Julie rang the bell, which made a light flash inside the house for Joy to see. Amanda hung back, and Alison and Angela shuffled nervously behind Julie.

Joy opened the door. "Julie! Come on in. What are you—" Then her face went white as she saw the other girls. She stood stiffly, with the door half-open.

"It's okay," said Julie, reaching for Joy's hand. Joy pulled back as if she'd been burned.

"Joy, please let us in," said Angela, stepping forward. "We just want to talk to you."

"We came to say we're sorry," said Alison, rubbing her heart with her fist. Angela and Amanda quickly joined in.

Joy's dark eyes welled up as she opened the door wider.

Sitting on the floor around the coffee table in the front room, the Water Fountain Girls told Joy how sorry they were. Julie could see in their faces that they meant it, and she knew Joy could see it, too.

Joy's mother came in with mugs of hot chocolate, and soon the room was filled with chatter and signing.

"What I don't get is how did the three of you learn all this sign language?" asked Joy, her forehead crinkling.

Julie told Joy about the new detention.

"And it really worked!" said Alison and Angela at the same time. All the girls laughed.

When it was time to go, the girls brought their mugs into the kitchen and thanked Mrs. Jenner.

On their way out the door, Alison turned to Julie. "What's the sign for *friend*?"

Julie showed her how to hook index fingers to say *friend* in sign language. Alison reached over and hooked her finger with Joy's. As they locked fingers together, a fleeting trace of a smile passed over Joy's face, like sun peeking through a cloud.

❖

On Monday morning, Julie and Joy walked to school together. Even though it was election day and Julie was anxious, at least Joy was back at school. No matter what happened, they'd face it together.

As they entered the school, Julie saw T. J. at the edge of a crowd of students. He waved, but instead of coming over, he turned and called, "They're here!" The crowd parted, and there in the middle of the front lobby stood the Water Fountain Girls, dressed from head to toe in green and blue, the school colors.

"From the top. One, two, three!" called Angela

as she, Amanda, and Alison led the crowd in a song:

If you're happy and you know it, vote for Julie.
If you're happy and you know it, jump for Joy.
If you're happy and you know it,
Then your VOTE will really show it.
If you're happy and you know it …
VOTE FOR JULIE! JUMP FOR JOY!

Everybody clapped and cheered.

Joy touched the tips of both hands to her mouth and extended them out in gratitude, signing *thank you* to the three girls.

"Wow, thanks, you guys!" said Julie. "That was really neat."

"Yeah, I wish I'd thought of it," said T. J., "but they came up with it on their own. Isn't it great? Now lots of people are saying they're going to vote for you guys."

Julie looked around. Students were humming the catchy tune as they drifted off to their lockers and classes. Her opponent, Mark, was nowhere to be seen.

✽

It took all day for each classroom to vote and for Mr. Arnold to tally the results. Julie caught herself staring at the loudspeaker on the wall, willing it to call them down to the assembly where Mr. Arnold would announce the winner. At last, the familiar crackle came over the PA system, and Julie heard the vice principal's voice.

"Students, we have the results of the election that you've all been waiting to hear. Starting with grade one, please make your way down to the gymnasium as quietly as possible."

As soon as they were seated, Julie asked Joy, "What's the sign for *butterflies*?"

Joy crossed her hands, linking her thumbs and wiggling her fingers. Julie made the sign for *butterflies* and then pointed to her stomach to show Joy how nervous and excited she felt.

Joy gave her a thumbs-up, wishing her good luck.

Mr. Arnold stepped up to the podium. "In all my years as head of student government, this has been one of the most exciting school elections at

Jack London Elementary. All the candidates did an outstanding job and certainly gave us a lot to think about. There can only be one winner today, but everyone who participated in the election is a winner."

A first grader in the front row blurted out, "Teacher, who won? The boy or the girl?" The students burst out in laughter.

Mr. Arnold smiled. "To answer that question—" he paused for dramatic effect, and then went on— "I would like to extend my sincere congratulations to the 1976 Jack London Elementary student body president and vice president, Miss Julie Albright and Miss Joy Jenner! Please join me on the stage." The audience erupted with applause.

Julie and Joy hugged each other and then ran up the steps onto the stage to shake hands with Mr. Arnold. When the applause died down, the students in Class 5D suddenly rose to their feet, a small oasis in the center of the audience. Their hands, like fluttering leaves, waved in silent celebration as they applauded in sign language.

Looking out over the sea of teachers, classmates, and friends, Julie thought about all the changes the past year had held for her—a new school, a new home, and hardest of all, a new way of being a family. She smiled wistfully, remembering how hard it had been, at first, to stop wishing things would somehow go back to the way they used to be. But over the past year, she had learned that she didn't have to be afraid of change. It was different, and it was sometimes sad, even painful—but it was also an invitation to think new thoughts, to see things in a new way, to grow. Even to become a better person.

And all the changes had brought her to this moment—student body president.

Suddenly, T. J. dashed up onto the stage and yanked on a dangling rope. Bright balloons and confetti fluttered down, magically swirling around her.

"T. J., how on earth did you pull that off?" Julie asked him, laughing.

"Oh, Mr. Arnold and I had it all planned, no matter who won. But I had my fingers crossed that it would be you." He batted at a balloon and gave her a cocky grin. "This is how they do it for real when the president gets elected. One day that's going to be me—campaign manager for the president of the United States."

"You're hired!" said Julie. "When I run for president someday, there's nobody I'd rather have running my campaign."

LOOKING BACK

CHANGES FOR AMERICA
IN THE
1970s

In the fall of 1976, when Julie's story ends, many Americans saw the presidential election as an opportunity for change. In schools, children like Julie followed the campaigns of the two candidates. President Gerald Ford and former Georgia governor Jimmy Carter had different ideas about how the country should be run. Ford had more political experience than Carter. But

Many African Americans supported Carter, who had governed successfully in Georgia, a state with a large black population.

because he had been Nixon's vice president, Ford was closely linked to President Nixon's failings. Many Americans felt Carter represented a change in leadership and a new direction for America.

When Jimmy Carter was elected president, the nation faced a number of difficult challenges. High *inflation*—an increase in the price of goods and services— made it harder for people to afford the things they needed.

1976 Chevette.
A new kind of American car.

American auto makers began offering models to compete with the small, light Japanese cars, which cost less and got better mileage than the big American "gas guzzlers."

At the same time, thousands of American workers lost their jobs as U.S. companies moved overseas, where workers could be hired for less. And increased competition from foreign companies, especially in cars and electronics, hurt American companies and workers.

One of the biggest issues during Carter's presidency was the *energy crisis*, a worldwide oil shortage that led to high heating costs and gas prices. Carter encouraged Americans to start using other energy sources—such as coal, wind, solar, or nuclear power. He also encouraged people to do what they could to *conserve*, or save energy. These issues are still with us today.

GAS SHORTAGE! Sales Limited to 10 GALS. OF GAS. PER CUSTOMER

Service stations had to ration, or restrict, *gas sales.*

During the oil shortage, people often had to wait in line for hours at gas stations to fill up their tanks. Many

carpooled, rode bikes, or walked to save gas. With car travel limited, families spent more of their leisure time at home. People looked to their favorite pastimes, like watching television, as a way

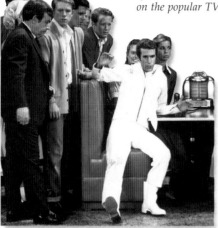

to forget the hard times. Television shows set in the 1950s—like *Happy Days* and *Laverne & Shirley*, which looked back at America's recent past as a simpler and happier time— were hugely popular with both children and parents.

Yet, as appealing as it was to think back on a time when life seemed easier, many Americans would not have wanted to go back to the way life was in the 1950s. They were grateful for the social changes that had taken place since then. Among the biggest changes were efforts to give women and minorities the same opportunities in education and jobs that white men had always had.

As a result of these social changes, more women and African Americans began to run for elected office. One of the more prominent politicians of the 1970s was Shirley

The ERA, or Equal Rights Amendment, said that the U.S. Constitution applied to women as well as men. But although Congress passed it, not enough states approved it to amend the Constitution.

Chisholm, the first African American woman to be elected to the U.S. Congress. Chisholm ran as a

Shirley Chisholm

In 2007, California Congresswoman Nancy Pelosi became the first woman Speaker of the House of Representatives. Here she is sworn in as her grandchildren watch.

Democratic candidate in the 1972 presidential election. Although she didn't win, she showed the nation that women—including women of color—could seriously be considered as candidates.

The 1970s also brought positive change for people with disabilities. For years, people with disabilities could

A 1975 law enabled students of different abilities to attend school together.

not go to regular schools or get jobs, making it hard for them to live independent lives. Children who were blind or deaf like Joy or who had other disabilities usually didn't attend the same schools or classes as other children. One girl, Judy Heumann, who used a wheelchair, sensed that her classmates felt awkward around her and viewed her as "the girl in the wheelchair." In 1970, at age 22, Judy started a group called Disabled in Action to raise awareness and fight for the rights of people with disabilities. She wanted to change people's attitudes and show that

As girls, actress Marlee Matlin, left, and 1995 Miss America Heather Whitestone, right, were teased for being deaf—but didn't let it stop them! Heather is signing "I love you."

having a disability didn't mean you couldn't lead a productive life. Thanks to activists like Judy, new laws were passed to give people with disabilities greater access to the world around them.

The desire to make the world a better place—which Julie shows in her stories and many real Americans shared during the 1970s—is still alive today. Together, children and grown-ups work hard to improve their schools, protect the environment, and help others in need. While the country still faces many of the problems it did in Julie's time, Americans of all ages, races, abilities, and political viewpoints continue to tackle these issues with optimism and creativity. They don't always agree with one another, but they usually share the same basic goal—to make their country truly a place of justice, freedom, and equality.

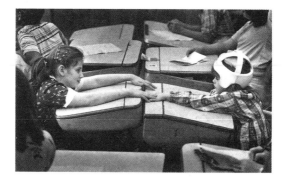

A SNEAK PEEK AT

GOOD LUCK, *Ivy*

Ivy Ling loves gymnastics. Her skills are improving, and she'll be a key team member at the all-city tournament—if she can overcome her fear of the balance beam.

For Ivy, the best time of the day was when school got out. Every afternoon, she would hurry to the Chinatown YWCA to practice with the rest of the Twisters gymnastics team.

"Girls, please gather around!" Coach Gloria was young and pretty. Her thick brown hair was tied in a ponytail, and she wore several rubber bands on her wrist in case anyone forgot hers. "Win or lose, after this year's all-city competition, we're having a big party!"

"Oooo! Can we have pizza?" Susie asked.

"Well, that's up to all of you. We're going to need a fund-raiser for our party. Any suggestions?"

"A lemonade stand?" said Cindy.

"Or a car wash?" said Karen.

"What about a bake sale?" Jennifer suggested.

Everyone began talking at once, and soon it was decided. The Twisters gymnastics team bake sale would take place that weekend.

Ivy's hand shot up in the air. "I'll bring my mom's famous Chinese almond cookies!" Soon everyone was volunteering brownies and cupcakes and other treats.

"This all sounds great," Coach Gloria said. "But

now it's time for practice. The all-city tournament is coming up fast!"

Ivy pulled her black hair into a short ponytail and then did her stretches before taking her position on the mat. As always, the minute Ivy heard the music, she relaxed and began her floor exercise routine. Her body loved doing the flips and twists and turns. Her mother always said that even when she was a baby, she was tumbling all over the living room.

"Your floor work's looking good, Ivy," Coach Gloria noted. "Are you ready to get on the beam?"

Ivy gulped. Her coach expected the girls to master the floor exercise, the vault, the uneven bars, and the balance beam. In the past, Ivy had done well in the all-around competition. That is, until the tournament before last. No matter how hard she tried to shake the incident out of her mind, she couldn't.

Ivy had just mounted the balance beam, smiling confidently. As she went through her mandatory movements—split jump, pivot, tuck jump—her body moved exactly as it was supposed to. Then, as she began a back walkover, she felt herself wobble. Panic shot through her as she struggled to regain her balance. But it was too late. Ivy could hear the crowd gasp as

Ivy had just mounted the balance beam, smiling confidently.

she hit the cushioned mat with a thud.

Her shoulder hurt and her legs were shaking as she got up. Ten seconds, ten seconds. Ivy knew she had only ten seconds to get back on the beam or risk more point deductions. Her hands were sweaty and her arms felt weak. She tried to get back on the beam but slipped and fell again. Then the tears began. She couldn't turn them off. Mortified, she ran away and hid in the girls' bathroom, unable to face the judges, the audience, or her team.

Trying to push the memory out of her mind, Ivy slowly approached the balance beam. The beam was sixteen feet long, four inches wide, and four feet off the ground. It seemed miles high.

"Are you still feeling unsure of yourself?" Coach Gloria asked.

Ivy bit her lip. "A little."

"Try to set your fears aside, and give it your best shot."

Ivy took a deep breath and lifted herself onto the beam.

"Okay, let's go, Ivy!" she heard her coach saying.

"Flat foot, lift your back leg higher, Ivy!

"Ivy, you lost your line. Don't drop that leg!

"Plié, jump straight up. Again—higher!"
I can't do anything right, Ivy scolded herself.
With each move she felt as if she was losing
control. Ivy couldn't look at her coach.

"Okay, let's take a break," Coach Gloria
finally said.

Ivy exhaled and jumped off the beam.

"You know that Olga Korbut won an
Olympic gold medal in balance beam," said Coach
Gloria.

"And gold in floor, too," added Ivy.

Coach Gloria smiled. "She helped her team win
gold as well. She's why you're here, right?"

Ivy nodded. She could still recall her
family crowded around the TV set four
years ago, watching the petite Russian
gymnast compete in the Olympics.
Even though Ivy had been only
six years old at the time, she was
mesmerized. At that moment she
dreamed of becoming a gymnast like
Olga Korbut. Later that fall, Ivy started lessons.

Olga Korbut

"Olga can do backward aerial somersaults with
her eyes closed," Ivy mumbled. "I can't even stay on

the balance beam."

"When she introduced that move at the Munich Olympics," her coach began, "it might have been the first time the world saw it, but it wasn't the first time Olga had tried it. She practiced and practiced and practiced to make it look so easy." Coach Gloria looked into Ivy's eyes. "You have a natural talent, Ivy. All you need to do is push past your fear."

Practice, practice, practice, Ivy said to herself. *Practice, practice, practice.*

✿